CONFESSIONS OF A GYM-CLASS DROPOUT

A PLAY BY
CHUCK RANBERG AND PATRICK DALEY

SCHOLASTIC INC.
New York   Toronto   London   Auckland   Sydney
Mexico City   New Delhi   Hong Kong

COVER ILLUSTRATION BY

JOHN C. WARD

INTERIOR ILLUSTRATIONS BY

PETER SPACEK

CONFESSIONS OF A GYM-CLASS DROPOUT was originally published as
"Ultrabodies" in *Scholastic Action®* magazine, Vol. 15, No. 14, May 1, 1992.

ISBN 0-439-05693-4

5   6   7   8   9   10   23   06   05   04

CHARACTERS

Travis Underwood - a kid

Narrator - older Travis

Mr. Underwood - Travis's father

Ralph - Travis's friend

Rocco - a big bodybuilder

Coach Willis - the gym coach

Al B. - a trainer at the YMCA

Sheryl - Travis's girlfriend

Felicia - Rocco's girlfriend

Travis's gym class

Travis Underwood is not exactly in the best shape—not yet, anyway.

Narrator: I always liked gym class, except for two things: the semi-annual physical fitness tests, and the guys who never washed their gym clothes.

Coach Willis: Hello, you good-for-nothing wimps! Today we're testing to see how many pull-ups you can do.

Narrator: Make that three things. Our gym coach was kind of like one of those evil prison guards you see in old movies. Only Coach Willis is not nearly as nice as some of those guards.

Coach Willis: Hurry up, Underwood, you wimp! You're next.

Narrator: Coach Willis always called everyone a wimp. He probably thought it gave him a tough-guy image.

Travis: Okay, Coach. Here I go.

Narrator: I jumped and grasped the pull-up bar, imagining I was an Olympic gymnast going for the gold. I could almost hear the roar of the crowd as I strained to pull my chin over the bar.

Travis: Uuuuuuuugh!

Narrator: That was one.

Travis: Urrrrrrrrrrgh!

Narrator: Two.

Travis: Aaaaaaah!

Narrator: Two and a half. Yep, that was it. With all eyes on me, I fell to the floor after two and a half pull-ups. My face was red. I was gasping for air. And my hands hurt as if I had been gripping cut glass. It was *not* a pretty sight.

Coach Willis: That's pitiful, Underwood. Next time take those rocks out of your pockets. Ha ha.

Travis: Yeah. Okay, Coach.

Narrator: Coach Willis thought he had a sense of humor, but he was mistaken.

Rocco: Out of the way, Underwood. Why don't you let a man go next?!

Narrator: That was Ed Rocovitch, whom everybody called Rocco. Rocco was built like a tank in tennis shoes. To say he was into bodybuilding would be like saying John Elway plays a little football. This guy was *serious*. He was also a jerk, the kind of guy who'd enjoy kicking sand in your face, even indoors.

Travis: Lay off, Rocco. I did my best. Not everyone can do as many pull-ups as you can.

Rocco: With those pipe-cleaner arms and that marshmallow body, I'm amazed you can even lift a fork to your face!

Narrator: The rest of the class laughed, and I tried not to look too embarrassed. Coach Willis beamed. He thought Rocco was really funny.

Coach Willis: Come on, Rocco. Show these wimps how it's done.

Narrator: Rocco walked over to the pull-up bar. I was hoping he'd get a cramp, or that the bar would break, or that his shorts would fall down.

Coach Willis: Come on, big guy! You're doing great!

Narrator: You could always tell who was one of Coach Willis' favorite students. He would always call them "big guy." I, of course, was always called "wimp."

Coach Willis: That's it, big guy! Keep going!

Narrator: Rocco continued to chin himself as if he were weightless. Eighteen, 19, 20 . . . Hadn't we been humiliated enough? Twenty-three, 24, 25. Finally, he stopped and grinned at us. He wasn't even breathing hard.

Rocco: Top that, ladies!

Narrator: Of course no one could. Rocco went to Ultrabodies, the best gym in town. He considered himself too advanced to use the weight lifting equipment at school. He always wore his Ultrabodies T-shirt in gym class, just in case we forgot. You could really hate a guy like that. I know I did.

Travis had to admit that maybe Rocco was right. Maybe he was a little on the wimpy side.

Narrator: That night, at home, I took my shirt off and stood in front of a mirror. Rocco's words still stung. My body wasn't that bad, but I guess I had let myself get out of shape. My arms were thin, even when I made a muscle, and my stomach was a little soft, except when I held my breath. I had to do something. My honor was at stake.

Mr. Underwood: What are you doing, Travis? Practicing to be a centerfold?

Narrator: Geez! Why do parents always embarrass you at your weakest moments?

Travis: No, Dad. Nothing. I'm doing nothing.

Narrator: I tried to change the subject. Uh, Dad, could you give me a lift to Java Joe's tonight?

Mr. Underwood: Is your homework done?

Travis: Of course it is, Dad.

Narrator: Well, most of it, anyway.

Mr. Underwood: Sorry, Travis, I'm low on gas.

Narrator: Dad liked to toy with my emotions.

Travis: We could stop by a gas station on the way. I'll pump. Please? Sheryl and I are supposed to meet Ralph.

Narrator: Sheryl was my girlfriend. She went to another school, so I didn't get to see her that often. Ralph was a friend of ours. He worked behind the counter at Java Joe's, which was a popular hangout.

Mr. Underwood: Okay, Travis. But when you want a ride home, make sure you call at a reasonable hour.

Travis: Sure thing, Dad. Thanks.

Narrator: Sometimes Dad could be nice. You just never knew when.

Do you think Rocco's comments are bugging Travis? Why or why not?

Another piece of pie? Another milkshake? Well, maybe not. . . .

ACT 3

Narrator: Later that evening, I met Sheryl and Ralph at Java Joe's.

Travis: Sheryl, what are you doing this summer?

Sheryl: I don't know. I was thinking about starting a car wash. Why?

Ralph: Hey there, you two. Another milkshake, another piece of pie?

Travis: Sure. Ralph, do you know what makes the pie here so good?

Ralph: That's Java Joe's secret recipe. But between you and me and the wall . . .

Sheryl: Yes?

Ralph: I think he sneezes in the filling.

Sheryl: Ralph, that's gross!

Ralph: Hey, reality hurts. What're you guys up to?

Sheryl: We're talking about the summer. Do you have any plans yet?

Ralph: Sure. I plan to keep working here, followed by a long life of more of the same. How about you?

Travis: I'm thinking of joining Ultrabodies.

Ralph: Ultrabodies?! The gym where Rocco pumps iron?!

Travis: Well, I didn't do so well on the last gym test, and I think I need to get in shape.

Narrator: I decided to leave the humiliation part out of the story.

Sheryl: You're not in bad shape, Travis.

Ralph: Not at all. I always tell everyone that you're the Bo Jackson of couch potatoes.

Sheryl: I think Travis is just fine the way he is.

Travis *(to Sheryl)*: That's why you're such a wonderful person, and *(to Ralph)* you're not.

Ralph: Hey, reality—

Travis: I know, reality hurts.

Narrator: At that moment reality walked through the door. It was Rocco. He was with his girlfriend,

Felicia, the former love of my life and the most beautiful girl on the planet. The fact that she preferred a guy like Rocco to me only proved how shallow she was. I kept reminding myself of that, and sometimes I even believed it.

Ralph (*rudely*): Oh look. It's Fred and Wilma, the sweetest couple on earth.

Narrator: They sat in a corner booth. I sneaked a few glances at them. Felicia drank a diet drink and Rocco had the "usual"—skim milk and the fresh fruit platter. How could he eat that stuff? Rocco looked up suddenly, and I pretended to be studying the overhead lights. They were dirty. I saw Rocco lean over and whisper something to Felicia, and she laughed.

Ralph: More pie, Travis?

Travis: No thanks, Ralph. Just the check.

Why do you think Travis is thinking about joining Ultrabodies?

Travis needs a little extra money, and his dad needs a little extra yard work done.

Narrator: School was ending, and it was time to discuss my training program with Dad. I knew that since money was involved, I had to be smart.

Travis: Dad, I've decided that I need to get in shape this summer.

Mr. Underwood: Oh, really? Good for you.

Travis: I want to improve my gym scores and build up my muscles. I think it will also be good for my self-confidence.

Narrator: Dad was always a sucker for words like "self-confidence."

Mr. Underwood: That sounds great, Travis. I know just what you can do.

Travis: You do?

Mr. Underwood: There's a lot of yard work that needs to be done around here. . . .

Narrator: Hold the phone!

Travis: Uh, Dad? I was thinking more along the lines of joining a gym, like Ultrabodies.

Mr. Underwood: A gym?

Travis: Yeah. So I could get a real, professional workout. There's this jock in my class named Rocco who gets on my case, and I thought if I could just beat him at one thing, like pull-ups, he'd lay off me. . . .

Narrator: . . . And find someone else to insult . . .

Travis: . . . And so I want to join Ultrabodies because it's the best gym in town. They have summer memberships for the low, low price of 300 dollars . . .

Mr. Underwood: Three hundred dollars?!

Narrator: I guess I should have worked that in a little slower.

Mr. Underwood: Out of the question, Travis. When I was your age, blah, blah, blah, blah . . .

Narrator: I'm sorry, but whenever Dad started a sentence with, "When I was your age . . ." I tuned him out.

Travis: I understand, Dad.

Narrator: Oh well. No gym. There went my dreams of shutting up Coach Willis. There went my fantasies of saying, "in your face" to Rocco. There went my image of my new "ultra-body."

Mr. Underwood: . . . But if you'll help with the yard work I'll give you the money to join the gym at the YMCA.

Travis: You will? Thanks, Dad! I knew I could count on you!

Are those workout machines for torturing people—or for getting them in shape?

Act 5

Narrator: The YMCA had been around for years, but their equipment was in good shape. Also, the staff had their act together—fortunately for me. I'd never used any workout machines. When I walked into the room and saw them, I got sort of nervous. To me they looked like modern torture devices, not like bodybuilding equipment. It turned out they were both. On my first day, a guy on staff showed me how to use everything.

Al B.: Hi. I'm Al B. Don't ask me what the "B" stands for.

Travis: Okay, I won't. I'm Travis Underwood.

Al B.: Is this your first time in a gym?

Travis: Does it show?

Al B.: Don't worry about it. Take this card. As we go from machine to machine, we'll write down how much you can lift. That way you can keep a

record of your progress as time goes by.

Narrator: Each machine concentrated on one muscle group: biceps, triceps, quadriceps, abdominals—we worked them all. When it got hard, I imagined I was a wrestler, facing Rocco in the ring, picking him up over my head and slamming him down on his ugly—

Al B.: Hey don't strain so much, man! It's only your first day!

Travis: But I want to build up. Don't they say "No pain, no gain"?

Al B.: Yeah, they also say "No gain if you injure yourself!" You gotta learn how to listen to your body. Pay attention to what it tells you.

Travis: Okay. How often should I work out?

Al B.: That depends. What's your goal?

Narrator: The total destruction of Rocco.

Travis: Oh, just all-around fitness.

Al B.: Then you should work out at least three times a week. How's your diet?

Narrator: I told him that at that very moment I was craving a bacon cheeseburger and fries from Java Joe's. Al B. shook his head.

Al B.: Very bad, man. Very bad. Knock off foods with high fat or sugar. Think carbos—carbohydrates, like pasta. And think fresh fruit and vegetables.

Travis: I hate those things!

Al B.: Hey, I don't make the rules. You want results or not?

Narrator: Yes, I wanted results. So I shut up. This was going to be harder than I thought. All of a sudden I had a little respect for how hard Rocco worked on his body. But of course, you have to work on your body when you don't have a brain!

Do you think Al B. will be able to help Travis? Do you think Travis will stick with Al B.'s program?

OUCH!!!!

Act **6**

Narrator: The next morning, I must say that I *really* felt the work-out.

Mr. Underwood: Hey, Travis, time to get up! You promised to help me repair the fence today.

Travis: I'd be glad to, Dad. It's just that I can't seem to move.

Narrator: Every muscle in my body ached from working out. Does Arnold Schwarzenegger have days like this?

Mr. Underwood: Come out to the garage when you're dressed. I want to show you something.

Travis: Okay, ouch, Dad. I'll just put on my, ouch, T-shirt and, ouch, jeans. Or maybe I'll just put on a—ouch!—body cast.

Narrator: I checked myself out in the mirror. To justify all this pain I deserved to look like

Sylvester Stallone. I looked the same. Sigh. I limped out to the garage.

Mr. Underwood: I was at the hardware store, and I thought that, well, maybe you could use something like this.

Narrator: He pointed to a shiny bar in the doorway between the garage and the house.

Travis: A pull-up bar?

Mr. Underwood: Yes. Didn't you say you wanted to set a record or something?

Narrator: I didn't always think Dad listened to me, but I guess he heard the important things.

Why do you think Mr. Underwood installed the pull-up bar in the garage?

What? More exercise?! Travis finds out that with Al B., the fun never ends!

Act 7

Narrator: The first few weeks were painful, but I kept up my program three times a week. Pretty soon my muscles didn't hurt quite as much. And I could already do six pull-ups!

Al B.: What kind of aerobics do you do?

Travis: Aerobics?

Al B.: Yeah, you know—jogging, swimming, bike riding, Jane Fonda videos . . .

Travis: I have to do aerobics, too?

Narrator: Just when I thought I was safe!

Al B.: I'm afraid so, man. To burn fat and work on your cardiovascular system, you gotta do more.

Travis: Swell.

Al B.: Hey, don't be discouraged, man. You've made great progress. This means it's time to move to the next level.

Could it be that Travis's hard work is finally starting to pay off?

Act 8

Narrator: So I started doing laps in the pool at the YMCA. First I swam for ten minutes. Then I worked up to 30 minutes. At sunset I'd go for long bike rides. Sometimes Sheryl would join me if she wasn't too tired from working at her car wash, which was making a lot of money. We'd always end up at Java Joe's.

Ralph: What'll you crazy kids have tonight? I recommend the pecan pie—only two sneezes.

Sheryl: Gross. I'll have a chocolate shake, hold the sneezes, Ralph.

Ralph: And the usual for you, Arnold?

Travis: Yeah, thanks.

Ralph: As you wish, one fresh fruit plate. Would you like some bacon grease on the side?

Travis: Tempting, but no thanks.

Narrator: Actually, I was really starting to *like* the fresh fruit plate.

Ralph: Don't look now, but here comes what's-her-name.

Narrator: Sure enough, Felicia had come in alone. She looked around to see if any of her gang was there. Then she decided to head for the counter. I pretended not to notice her.

Felicia: Hi, Travis.

Narrator: I nearly choked on a peach pit.

Travis: Uh, hi, Felicia. What're you doing?

Felicia: Just hanging out. Rocco's at some jock festival somewhere.

Narrator: Oh? Was it possible her life without me wasn't perfect? I tried not to be smug.

Travis: Felicia, this is my girlfriend, Sheryl.

Narrator: Okay, maybe just a little smug.

Felicia: Hi, Sheryl.

Sheryl: Hi, Leslie.

Felicia: Uh, that's *Felicia.*

Sheryl: Oh, sorry.

Felicia: Well, I have to go now. Nice seeing you, Travis. You're looking really good these days.

Travis: You too, Felicia.

Narrator: I was not a fool, and so I quickly turned to Sheryl.

Travis: But not as good as you, Sheryl.

Sheryl: Hmph!

Narrator: Did Felicia, the homecoming-queen-in-training, really think I was "looking good"? Was she paying attention to me now merely because I'd been going to the gym? I guess she was as shallow as I had thought. Excellent!

After a summer of feeling the burn, Travis faces Coach Willis's pull-up contest.

Narrator: September again. Time to return to reading, writing, and the ranting of Coach Willis. But this time I knew that I was ready. This time I knew that I was in shape. This time I knew that I'd be respected!

Coach Willis: Welcome back, wimps!

Narrator: Maybe *respect* was a little too much to hope for.

Coach Willis: Let's see how all you worthless slobs perform on the chin-up bar after sitting around all summer!

Narrator: He didn't scare us as much as he thought. We had all heard rumors that he spent his summers growing tulips.

Coach Willis: So far this week you've proven you can't run or do sit-ups any better than last year.

Narrator: Actually, I had improved at sit-ups and running, and Rocco had been perfect as usual.

Coach Willis: Now let's see how bad you are at pull-ups!

Narrator: The moment of truth. Thanks to Al B.'s coaching and my home pull-up bar, I had worked myself up to 22 pull-ups. With a little luck I knew I could equal Rocco's number, and maybe do one or two for insurance. I couldn't beat him at any other sports. But at least this would be one small victory for the wimps of the world!

Coach Willis: You're next, Underwood. And remember, half a pull-up doesn't count!

Narrator: Tulip grower!

Travis: Right. Don't worry, Coach.

Narrator: My mouth was dry. All the moisture had gone to my hands. I wiped them on my shirt, then jumped up to grab the bar. This was it!

Coach Willis *(counting)*: That's one, that's two, that's three . . .

Narrator: At least he could count. The first ten came easily.

Coach Willis: Ten, 11! Good, Underwood!

Narrator: What was this? Actual encouragement?

Coach Willis: Fourteen, 15!

Narrator: Now each one was getting harder. This was what would separate the men from the . . . well, wimps.

Travis: Uhh!

Coach Willis: Nineteen!

Narrator: My heart was pounding. My biceps were aching. Twenty! Twenty-one! I tried not to grunt too loudly.

Travis *(loudly)*: Augh!

Coach Willis: Twenty-two! Go for it!

Narrator: How did my body get so heavy? My arms felt like they were suddenly made of spaghetti. I thought of wiping the grin off Rocco's face, of making him regret the day he ever mocked Travis Underwood. . . . I did another one. The whole class started to count along!

The Class: Twenty-three!

Travis: UHH!

The Class: Twenty-four!

Travis: AAAAAAAAH!

The Class: Twenty-five!

Travis: OOOMF! YES!

Narrator: I did it! I dropped to the ground, hoping I wouldn't fall over. I tried to act as though my arms didn't feel like they were being pulled from their sockets.

Coach Willis: You've been working out, haven't you, Underwood?

Narrator: I tried not to gasp for breath.

Travis *(gasping)*: Well . . . yeah . . . a little . . .

Narrator: Nothing like a little fake modesty.

Coach Willis: Good going, Travis.

Narrator: Travis?! He called me Travis? He actually used my first name? This was a moment to enjoy!

Rocco: Not bad, geek face.

Narrator: Did I detect a note of nervousness in Rocco's voice? Was he suddenly a little less sure of himself? Was he possibly humbled that someone like me could equal him at something? Well, no, not quite.

Coach Willis: You're next, Rocco. Underwood is the one to beat.

Rocco: Watch me.

Narrator: Then Rocco wiped the floor with me, as they say. I guess he'd been working hard this summer, too. His final pull-up count was 36. That was high enough to prevent anyone else from even getting close.

Rocco: Top that, wuss!

Narrator: It didn't even make me feel better that he was sweating and gasping for air as he said, "Top that, wuss." The truth was, he'd beaten the sweatpants off me. I'd failed.

Why does Travis say that he has failed?
Do you think that he's right?

Al B. does some heavy lifting—of Travis's spirits.

Act **10**

Al B.: Twenty-five pull-ups?? Man! That is awesome! That is outstanding!

Travis: What's the difference? I still didn't beat that jerk Rocco.

Al B.: So? Look at yourself, man. Since you started coming here you've lost that inner tube around your middle and gained all this muscle. You went from a guy who couldn't chin himself on a towel rack to a guy who can do 25 with no problem. Give yourself some credit!

Travis: I guess that is pretty good, huh?

Al B.: No lie! And as long as you're giving out credit, it doesn't hurt to have a first-class trainer.

Travis: That's for sure. Thanks Al B.

Al B.: Hey, no problem.

Travis: Can I ask you something?

Al B.: Shoot.

Travis: What does the "B" stand for?

Al B.: Promise you won't tell anyone?

Travis: I swear.

Al B.: Bookbinder.

Travis: That's your last name? So what's wrong with that?

Al B.: Nothing, if you're a librarian. But would you take orders from a fitness trainer named Bookbinder?

Narrator: I had to agree with him. He was right about Rocco, too. It didn't matter that he could beat me with one bicep. I'd made myself stronger and healthier that summer, and now when I looked in the mirror I approved of what I saw. Still, a guy could always dream. . . .

Do you think Travis will continue going to the gym? Why or why not?